# Pirate Patch ★

## and the

# Chest of Bones

In which the bold
Pirate Patch and
Granny Peg finally put
to rest the infam...
Parr...

(...

For Lewis
R.I.

For Thomas
N.R.

Reading Consultant: Prue Goodwin, Lecturer in Literacy and
Children's Books at the University of Reading

ORCHARD BOOKS
338 Euston Road, London NW1 3BH
*Orchard Books Australia*
Hachette Children's Books
Level 17/207 Kent Street, Sydney NSW 2000

First published by Orchard Books in 2008
First paperback publication 2009

Text © Rose Impey 2008
Illustrations © Nathan Reed 2008

The rights of Rose Impey to be identified as the author and
Nathan Reed to be identified as the illustrator of this Work
have been asserted by them in accordance with the
Copyright, Designs and Patents Act, 1988.

A CIP catalogue record for this book is available from the British Library

ISBN 978 1 84362 976 4 (hardback)
ISBN 978 1 84362 984 9 (paperback)

1 3 5 7 9 10 8 6 4 2
Printed in China

Orchard Books is a division of Hachette Children's Books,
an Hachette Livre UK company.
www.hachettelivre.co.uk

# Pirate Patch

## and the

# Chest of Bones

ROSE IMPEY · NATHAN REED

ORCHARD BOOKS

Patch's mum and dad were
pirates. They were off sailing
on their pirate ship.
Patch wanted to be off
sailing, too . . .

But Granny Peg
was busy . . . digging.
When Peg had been a proper
pirate, she had buried treasure
all over the place. Now she
had forgotten where.

So every day she dug
a new hole.

Today she had dug up
a big pile of bones!
"Staggering Starfish!"
said Patch. "Whose
are those?"
Peg whispered, sadly,
"Pendragon's!"

Patch had heard of Peg's parrot. Pendragon had been the fiercest parrot ever to perch on a pirate's shoulder.

"This parrot deserves a proper burial at sea," sniffed Peg. "And I'm going to see he gets one."

Patch wasn't happy about that.
He wasn't exactly superstitious.
But even a little pirate knows
it's bad luck to sail with
a skeleton on board.

Patch, Portside and Pierre kept
a careful eye on that chest.

And when a terrible storm
hit the ship, they all knew
who was to blame.

Soon rain lashed their faces. Strong winds blew them miles off course.

THE LITTL

But worse was yet to come:
*The Little Pearl* hit a hidden
rock. In no time the ship
was almost underwater.

Patch began to think
*The Little Pearl* might be
doomed. But he was too
brave to admit it.

While Patch, Peg and Pierre
baled out the ship, Portside,
the cleverest sea dog ever to
sail the seven seas, made
a few running repairs.

At last the storm blew
over and *The Little Pearl*
was back on course.

Patch couldn't wait to get rid of those bones.

"What about here?" he asked.

But Peg wasn't happy until she had found the perfect spot. Finally she nodded and said, "Here!"

Pierre lowered the flag.
Portside played a final farewell,
while Peg made a short speech . . .
and then another . . .
and *another*.

THE LITTLE PEARL

22

As they lowered the chest overboard Peg wiped her eyes and sighed.

But Patch was looking over his shoulder. He spotted a small rowing boat.

When he looked through his
telescope, Patch saw their old
enemies: Bones and Jones.
The two pirates were fishing
*something* out of the water.

Patch didn't tell Peg. He smiled
as he waited to see what
would happen.

Patch knew that Bones and
Jones were probably the
*most* superstitious pirates
ever to sail the seven seas.

When they saw Pendragon's skeleton, they jumped right out of the boat.

"We're cursed!" yelled Bones,
"Doomed forever," howled Jones.

Back at home, Peg sighed.
"It does my heart good
to think of Pendragon's
bones safe at the
bottom of the sea."

Patch nodded,
and wisely
said . . . nothing.

# Pirate Patch

## ROSE IMPEY   NATHAN REED

All priced at £4.99

Orchard Colour Crunchies are available from all good bookshops,
or can be ordered direct from the publisher:
Orchard Books, PO BOX 29, Douglas IM99 1BQ
Credit card orders please telephone 01624 836000
or fax 01624 837033 or visit our internet site: www.orchardbooks.co.uk
or e-mail: bookshop@enterprise.net for details.

To order please quote title, author and ISBN
and your full name and address.
Cheques and postal orders should be made payable to 'Bookpost plc.'
Postage and packing is FREE within the UK
(overseas customers should add £2.00 per book).

Prices and availability are subject to change.